Four Friends Together

Sue Heap

WALKER BOOKS
AND SUBSIDIARIES
LONDON • BOSTON • SYDNEY

It's nearly time for the story.

Seymour the
sheep is ready ...

and Rachel the
rabbit is ready.

Mary Clare has the book
but she's fallen asleep.

"Yoo-hoo!" calls Florentina,
the great big flowery bear.

"Hello, my friends!"

"Look," says Florentina. "Little Mary Clare is asleep in my chair."

"We're going to have a story," says Rachel.

"It's nearly time," says Seymour.

Florentina fetches another chair.

"We have to be very quiet," says Rachel.

Florentina tries to sit on the chair.

She is too big.

"I'll try to be smaller,"
Florentina says.

"She's going to be smaller,"
Rachel says.

"How soon?" asks Seymour.

Mary Clare wakes up.

"Hello!" says Florentina.

"Florentina tried to be smaller!" says Rachel,

"but she's still big."

"Will you read the
story now?"

asks Seymour.

The four friends each sit in their own chairs.

"Once upon a time..." Mary Clare begins.

"It's no good for me," says Seymour.

"I can't see the pictures."

"Once upon a time..."
Mary Clare begins again.

"It's not just for you,
Seymour," says Rachel.
"It's for all of us."

"Once upon a time..." begins Mary Clare again.

"What about me?" says Florentina. "I feel all alone."

"Friends should be together," says Rachel.

And so...

Everyone sits in Florentina's lap
and Mary Clare starts the story again.
"Once upon a time, there were
four friends together..."

It is a very good story and
everyone can see the pictures.
They are all happy.